May we remember our elders even when they can no longer remember themselves.
—*M.Z.A.*

We live simultaneously in time and timelessness—just like our family recipes, passed on to the next generation with love.
—*C.T. & B.T.*

Copyright © 2025 by Something Will Emerge Productions, LLC. All rights reserved. No part of this book may be reproduced in any form without permission from the publisher.

ISBN: 978-1-68555-185-8
Ebook ISBN: 978-1-68555-426-2
Library of Congress Control Number: 2024913249

Illustrations by Chantelle and Burgen Thorne.
Edited by Cara Greene Epstein.
Art Direction by Rachel Lopez Metzger.

Manufactured in China.
1 3 5 7 9 10 8 6 4 2

The Collective Book Studio®
Oakland, California
www.thecollectivebook.studio

Tali and the Timeless Time

By Mira Z. Amiras

Illustrations by Chantelle and Burgen Thorne

THE collective BOOK STUDIO

"What does that mean, Nona?" I ask.

But she just gives me a great big hug and kisses me on the top of my head.

Then she gives my hands a great big squeeze and tells me that it's time for bed!

"I just got here, Nona!"

Nona thinks I need naps,
like I'm still little or something . . . .

I think she doesn't
understand time at all.
"It's Friday, Nona, and we
have so much to do instead!"

I think Nona loves naptime 'cause she needs to tell me stories, the same ones over and over. She tucks me in and starts a tale—
"I'm older, Nona, older!"

She's telling me "little girl" stories about my mama again.

Right now, it's Nona who needs to sleep a bit more. She won't mind while she's napping if I go outside to explore....

There's a fountain with angels in Nona's backyard with goldfish I check on and feed and help guard.

Today it's got a few leaves and flowers and twigs that dropped from the arbor right next to the figs.

I clean it all up and pour in extra water the way Nona told me that *her* nona taught her.

I'll show Nona what I did when she's more awake,
but we're both pretty hungry and when we're hungry . . .

We bake!
Today, it's bourekas, yummy for eating.
Nona makes them with filo
(which it turns out is cheating).
She says her nona let her
'cause it doesn't need kneading.

"Nona," I ask, "is it really okay to make bourekas all wrong?" But she says every family has secrets that they pass along....

She spreads out two filo leaves,
one on top of the other,
and tells me to brush them
with hot melted butter.
Then I dribble wilted spinach
and feta on top, roll into a cigar,
curl it, and fill the pan up.

Nona sprinkles on sesame
seeds, garlic, and pepper,
plus a kiss on my forehead
so I won't ever forget her.

Done.
Now we bake them.

With another kiss on my forehead, she calls me "Ramona"!

"Nona, I'm Tali, remember? *TALI!*"

She takes my hands and squeezes them tight, so I know everything's okay and she's really all right.

Sometimes my nona doesn't have words, but she can show me.

Last Friday we stuffed grape leaves, which Nona calls "yaprakas," or sometimes she says "dolma," and other times "dolmades."

We rolled them up tight
and cooked them in brine.
When they started to boil,
that was a good sign
that before very long
we'd be ready to dine.

But that wasn't in the Timeless Time.
That was just last week....

"The best dish of all," says Nona, "we call it just 'huevos'—that's 'eggs' in Ladino—cooked in a sauce of tomatoes, the Sefardi way with chunks of good feta. Sop it up with arroz or pan? Yum, even better!

"Nona, was that the Timeless Time— when Ladino was your language and it would have been mine?"

I'm having big thoughts, but Nona's not listening—

She's singing,
"'Chakchouka'
it's sometimes called,
not just huevos, in the
Holy Land, Tunisia, and
the land of the Pharaohs.
In Mexico, it's a lot like
huevos rancheros.
Chakchouka means
'all mixed up'—eggs
in tomatoes—"

Do these foods live in the Timeless Time, I wonder, since they're so ancient and have traveled all over?

Nona pinches my cheek and gives me a squeeze. She forgot that our cooking needs her expertise— now she's getting out her zills and her fans, I believe!

"Nona, it's Tali—we're cooking, Nona, cooking and baking. We're making our Shabbat dinner now, and I need you!"

"Come Nona sit down, sit down to our feast—dishes from the Mediterranean and the ancient Near East. Filo-bourekas, arroz, and huevos—the table's all set, y todos son buenos!"

Nona finally sits down toward the end of my visit. "Delicious!" she says, taking a bite—"but what *is* it?"

Then she picks up her zills and she hands me mine.

Maybe it's dancing that exists in the Timeless Time?

The sun has set and it's time to go home, but I'm not sure Nona should spend time alone.

"I love you, Nona," I tell her as she starts to snore.
"I'm so glad we live just right next door."

"Shabbat shalom," I whisper. "I love you, sweet dreams. May the animals guard you, the fountain fish and the trees."

I give her a kiss as they all entwine
and watch as they slip into the **Timeless Time** . . . .

Shhhhh . . .

Glossary

arroz Spanish and Ladino for "rice." Nona's arroz is sometimes called "Spanish rice"—a savory dish made with rice, tomato paste, onions, garlic, and a drizzle of olive oil.

boureka (börek) A delicious Sefardi pastry usually filled with spinach, cheese, or meat. Some make them in triangles, but we make them rolled up and twisted like cinnamon rolls, but savory. When stuffed with meat, they're yummy sprinkled with powdered sugar.

chakchouka (shakshuka) This Tunisian Arabic Berber word means "all mixed up"—and it is! Made of eggs poached in tomato sauce and spices, Sefardim often add feta cheese and spinach, yum. (see *huevos*)

filo (phyllo) A Greek name for thin sheets (or "leaves") of unleavened dough used for making both sweet and savory flaky pastries, like the bourekas Nona teaches Tali to make.

huevos (huevos b'tomat) Spanish and Ladino for eggs (and eggs in tomato). In Nona's family, huevos always means eggs stewed in tomatoes and cooked with feta.

nona (nonna) Ladino for grandmother, said with lots of love and hugs. "Nono" is grandfather—and while my nono doesn't feature in this story, I have amazing tales to tell about him as well!

pan/challah Pan is Spanish for bread, and challah is a delicious Jewish bread eaten on Shabbat. Breads are great for dipping in and enjoying Sefardi dishes, especially on holidays. Otherwise, arroz is served instead of bread.

Sefarad The ancient Hebrew word for Spain. It refers to the Jewish communities that lived there for centuries until they were expelled in 1492. Even though they were forced to leave, Sefardi Jews still take pride in their rich Sefardi heritage and culture.

Shabbat/Shabbat shalom From Friday sundown to Saturday sundown, Shabbat is celebrated every week by Jews around the world. It's a day for rest, giving thanks, and enjoying family time. No work—and no homework! "Shabbat shalom"—may you have a peaceful Shabbat!

yaprakas (dolma/dolmades) Stuffed grape leaves with fillings that can be either vegetarian or meat. The Ladino name comes from the Turkish word for "leaf"—yaprak. Dolma is the word for stuffing.

y todos son buenos A reassuring Spanish expression that means "and everything's fine!"

zills Turkish term for small metal finger cymbals used when singing and dancing to keep rhythm with the music. Zills make a bright, happy sound! I still have my nona's zills—and her Spanish castanets and fans!

Author's Note: There are three kinds of time: Linear time—events with dates, like history and pre-history. Circular time—where cycles repeat, like seasons. And timeless time—where all things are eternal, like myths, dreams, and secret family recipes.

This book is a love letter to my nona, whose house was filled with the eternal in the form of amazing smells, foods, music, and dance. "History is always now," my mother used to say, and many of our holidays celebrate events as if they are happening in the present. For my grandparents, Sefarad was eternal, as was the expulsion from Spain, and they would slip between the "now" that I perceived into that "eternal now" every time my grandfather picked up his oud or mandolin and my grandmother her castanets or zills. He would play ancient tunes and she would sing the ballads of old Sefarad—and they were home again. And so was I.

By the time I actually got to Spain, like my mother and grandmother, I already knew the streets and could find my way through the ancient Jewish quarters of Cordoba or Sevilla. My nona spoke to me in Ladino, but I answered her mostly in English. What a loss of language! Now that I'm a nona myself, I'm happy to pass on to you some of the good stuff, some of the hard stuff, and some of the timeless time I got to spend at Nona's house—just as my children and grandchildren now get to spend it with me.

Mira Z. Amiras is an anthropologist, author, and award-winning filmmaker. She received her Ph.D. from UC Berkeley and is professor emerita of Religion and Middle East Studies at SJSU. She is author of *Malkah's Notebook: A Journey into the Mystical Aleph-Bet*, the Tali children's books, and more. Mira lives in San Francisco with her family and furry four-legged friends.

Chantelle and Burgen Thorne, a multi–award winning illustration team, are eclectic bookworms who delight in the magic of stories. In the rolling green hills of South Africa they spend their days creating children's book art . . . and sometimes writing a story or two themselves. They're at their happiest drawing kids' stories with a bit of humor and a ton of animals. When not at their desks, they can be found being towed around the countryside by their two dogs.